# Dragons from Mars Go to School

By Deborah Aronson

Illustrated by Colin Jack

**HARPER**

*An Imprint of HarperCollinsPublishers*

Library of Congress Control Number: 2017943584

ISBN 978-0-06-236851-5

The artist used Photoshop and Sketchbook Pro to create the digital illustrations for this book.

19 20 21 22 23   SCP   10 9 8 7 6 5 4 3 2 1

❖

First Edition

To Justine, without a doubt
—Debbie

For Gabriel and Eli
—Dad

"Hurry up, Molly! Hurry up, Fred!
It's the first day of school!" Nathaniel said.
"Everyone knows that you flew here from Mars.
When they actually meet you,
they'll treat you like stars."

Molly was nervous and actually feared that the kids in the school might think they were weird.

"Maybe they've never seen dragons before.
What if they're frightened and run for the door?"

"They'll love you to pieces; they'll think you're just great.
Now hurry up, dragons, or we will be late!"

Over the treetops, together they flew.
Molly and Fred and Nathaniel, too.

When they got to the school, Molly said, "Gee, do they know we're the size of a huge SUV?

Will we fit in the doors?
Are they suitably wide?
Will we knock down the school?
Can we both squeeze inside?"

When they landed at school, the kids stared in awe,
shocked at the size of the dragons they saw.

The dragons could see that the doors were too small and they just couldn't fit in the building at all.

"Hold your breath, Molly. Hold your breath, Fred.
We'll get you inside," Nathaniel said.

So the dragons inhaled with all of their might,
and they got through the door, though it really was tight.

When they got to the classroom, they looked for a chair.
Molly said, "Fred, there's a chair over there."

When Fred tried to sit,
the chair fell apart.
Molly thought,
"Gee, this is not a good start."

Fred picked himself up and he straightened his hat.
The kids found him funny and teased him for that:

"Don't sit on the floor or you just might fall through!
Maybe you dragons should move to the zoo!"

"Now listen," said Molly. "I've heard quite enough.
We dragons can do some remarkable stuff:

We can rescue a kid
from the top of a tree.

She can slide down my tail
and be safe as can be.

"In art class, a dragon can really do lots.
Let's see . . . yes, of course . . . we can fire the pots!

"A quick trip to Mars? Does it sound like a blast?
We can fly you through space and we'll get you there fast.

"Do you want to shoot baskets like one of the pros?
Just take your best shot from the top of Fred's nose.

"If a school bus gets stuck and it needs to be towed,
we can give it a push and it's back on the road.

"And the planet of Mars is a place we know well.
Why not invite us to your show-and-tell?"

"We're sorry we laughed,"
said the kids in the school.
"We just didn't know that you
guys were so cool.
And we'd like to do something
to show that we care.
Would you like us to find you
a dragon-sized chair?"

Molly and Fred thought it over a bit.
"Can you widen the doorways so that we can fit?
And then, after that, once you've widened the doors,
you can join us in eating some dragon-fired s'mores!"

Molly and Fred were respected, admired.
"Will you come back tomorrow?" the children inquired.

The dragons did not even have to think twice.
"Of course we'll be back; that would be very nice."

Flying back home at the end of the day,
the dragons were happily winging their way.
Nathaniel was also enjoying the ride,
pleased with his dragons and beaming with pride.